Highlights Puzzle Readers

LEVEL 2

LET'S READ, READ, READ

Kit and Kaboodle

EXPLORE THE CITY

By Michelle Portice
Art by Mitch Mortimer

HIGHLIGHTS PRESS

Honesdale, Pennsylvania

Stories + Puzzles = Reading Success!

Dear Parents,

Highlights Puzzle Readers are an innovative approach to learning to read that combines puzzles and stories to build motivated, confident readers.

Developed in collaboration with reading experts, the stories and puzzles are seamlessly integrated so that readers are encouraged to read the story, solve the puzzles, and then read the story again. This helps increase vocabulary and reading fluency and creates a satisfying reading experience for any kind of learner. In addition, solving Hidden Pictures puzzles fosters important reading and learning skills such as:

- shape and letter recognition
- letter-sound relationships
- visual discrimination
- logic
- flexible thinking
- sequencing

With high-interest stories, humorous characters, and trademark puzzles, Highlights Puzzle Readers offer a winning combination for inspiring young learners to love reading.

This
is Kit.

This is
Kaboodle.

They love to travel.
You can help them on
each adventure.

As you read the story,
find the objects in each
Hidden Pictures
puzzle.

Then check the
Packing List on
pages 30-31 to make
sure you found everything.

Happy reading!

3

Kit and Kaboodle are visiting Sillyville.

"What can we do in the city?"
asks Kaboodle.

"Let's look at the map," says Kit.
"We can go to a museum.
We can go to a park.
We can go to a theater."

"Can we go to all three places?"
asks Kaboodle.

"Yes!" says Kit.

"This bus goes to all of them.

We have to be at the theater

by three o'clock.

That's when the show starts."

VILLE SNOOZE INN

ROOMS

TOUR STOP

"I hope I packed enough," says Kaboodle.

"I hope I did not pack too much," says Kit.

"Look at the sign," says Kaboodle.
"That's the tallest building in the city!"

"That building is on this postcard,"
says Kit.

"I packed a few things we can use
to send a postcard home," says Kaboodle.

He looks in his bag.

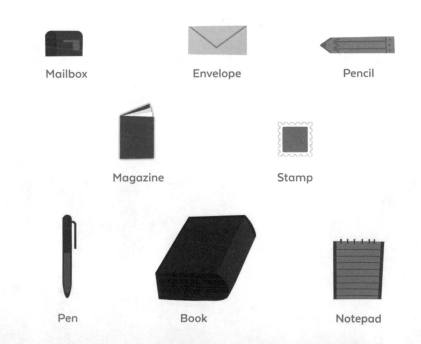

Mailbox   Envelope   Pencil

Magazine   Stamp

Pen   Book   Notepad

The bus stops in front of the museum.
Kit and Kaboodle get off the bus.

They buy tickets for the museum,
and then they go inside.

"We have plenty of time
before the show," says Kit.

"Look at the sign," says Kaboodle.
"This is the biggest museum in the city!"

"There's a lot to see here," says Kit.
"We might need to take a break."

"I packed a few things we can sit on,"
says Kaboodle.

He looks in his bag.

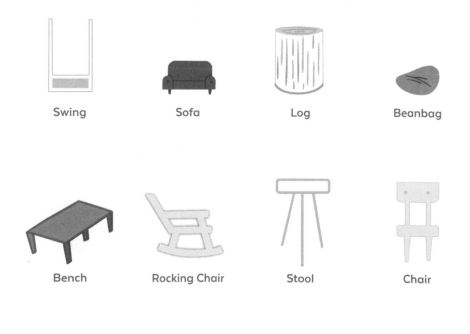

Swing   Sofa   Log   Beanbag

Bench   Rocking Chair   Stool   Chair

BIGGEST MUSEUM
IN SILLYVILLE!

GOOD BOY

13

"I like these paintings!" says Kit.

"Let's play a game," says Kaboodle.
"Which painting am I?"

"I found it!" says Kit.
"Which painting am I?"

"I found it!" says Kaboodle.

"Let's take a break and go outside," says Kit.
"We have plenty of time before the show."

"Look at the sign," says Kaboodle.
"This is the oldest park in the city!"

"Let's go play in the park," says Kit.

"I packed a few things we can play with,"
says Kaboodle.

He looks in his bag.

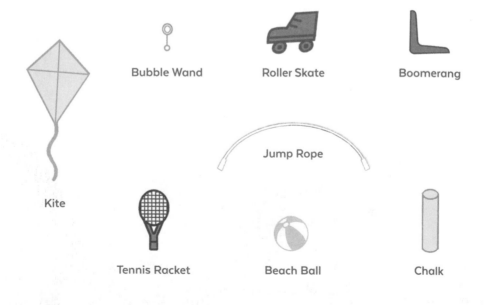

Bubble Wand

Roller Skate

Boomerang

Jump Rope

Kite

Tennis Racket

Beach Ball

Chalk

"Look at all the kites," says Kaboodle.

"The kites look like a rainbow in the sky!" says Kit.

"I see a purple kite with yellow stripes," says Kaboodle.

"I see a green kite with white dots," says Kit.

"What time is it?" asks Kit.
"We have to go to the theater.
The show starts at three o'clock!"

"I packed a few things
we can use to tell time,"
says Kaboodle.

He looks in his bag.

Potato Clock

Wristwatch

Hourglass

Phone

Calendar

Stopwatch

Timer

Clock

21

"Oh no!" says Kit.

"The show starts in 10 minutes!"

Kit and Kaboodle run to the theater.

They get there just in time!

Kit and Kaboodle find their seats.

The curtain opens and the show starts.

"What a great show!" says Kit.
"Let's get dinner from a food truck."

"I packed a few things
we can use to eat our dinner,"
says Kaboodle.

He looks in his bag.

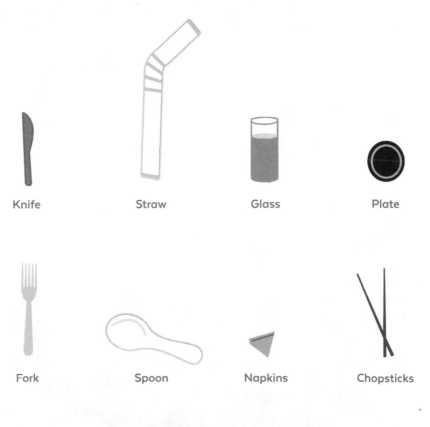

Knife

Straw

Glass

Plate

Fork

Spoon

Napkins

Chopsticks

"What a yummy dinner!" says Kit.

"I think we saw everything in Sillyville," says Kaboodle. "I'm tired."

"Let's go back to the hotel," says Kit.

Kit and Kaboodle hop back on the bus.

"Look!" says Kit. "There is the museum."

"There is the park," says Kaboodle.
"And there is the theater."

"I'm glad we made it to the show on time!"
says Kit.

"Sillyville is a great city to explore," says Kit.

"What a fun trip!" says Kaboodle.

"We make a good team," says Kit.

"Where should we go
on our next trip?" asks Kaboodle.

Bus

Canoe

Airplane

Rocket

Truck

Train

Sailboat

Car

Did you find all the things Kit and

Airplane

Beach Ball

Beanbag

Bench

Calendar

Canoe

Car

Chalk

Fork

Glass

Hourglass

Jump Rope

Mailbox

Napkin

Notebook

Pen

Rocket

Rocking Chair

Roller Skate

Sailboat

Stopwatch

Straw

Swing

Tennis Racket

Kaboodle packed for their trip?

Book	Boomerang	Bubble Wand	Bus
Chopsticks	Clock	Envelope	Chair
Kite	Knife	Log	Magazine
Pencil	Phone	Plate	Potato Clock
Sofa	Spoon	Stamp	Stool
Timer	Train	Truck	Wristwatch

For information about permission to reprint selections from this book,
please contact permissions@highlights.com.

Published by Highlights Press
815 Church Street
Honesdale, Pennsylvania 18431
ISBN (paperback): 978-1-64472-196-4
ISBN (hardcover): 978-1-64472-197-1
ISBN (ebook): 978-1-64472-242-8

Library of Congress Control Number: 2020934130
Manufactured in Melrose Park, IL, USA
Mfg. 09/2020

First edition
Visit our website at Highlights.com.
10 9 8 7 6 5 4 3 2 1

This book has been officially leveled by using the F&P Text Level
Gradient™ Leveling System.

LEXILE®, LEXILE FRAMEWORK® , LEXILE ANALYZER®, the LEXILE®
logo and POWERV® are trademarks of MetaMetrics, Inc., and are
registered in the United States and abroad. The trademarks and names
of other companies and products mentioned herein are the property of
their respective owners. Copyright © 2019 MetaMetrics, Inc.
All rights reserved.

For assistance in the preparation of this book, the editors would like
to thank Vanessa Maldonado, MSEd, MS Literacy Ed. K–12, Reading/LA
Consultant Cert., K–5 Literacy Instructional Coach; and Gina Shaw.